Przemysław Wechterowicz   Emilia Dziubak

HUG ME, PLEASE!

Text © 2013 Przemysław Wechterowicz, Emilia Dziubak
Illustration © 2013 Przemysław Wechterowicz, Emilia Dziubak
Translated by Przemysław Wechterowicz
This edition © 2018 Quarto Publishing plc

First Published in the English language in hardcover in 2017 by words & pictures,
an imprint of The Quarto Group.
The Old Brewery, 6 Blundell Street,
London N7 9BH, United Kingdom.
T (0)20 7700 6700 F (0)20 7700 8066
www.QuartoKnows.com

British Library Cataloguing in Publication Data available on request

ISBN: 978-1-91027-779-9

1 3 5 7 9 8 6 4 2

Manufactured in Dongguan, China TL012018

Przemysław Wechterowicz   Emilia Dziubak

HUG ME, PLEASE!

words & pictures

One morning, as the Sun was still brushing its teeth,
Little Bear and Daddy Bear went for a stroll.
"What shall we do today, Daddy?" Little Bear asked.
"Let's look for some honey!" Daddy Bear replied.

The honey was delicious. It gave them a warm, sweet feeling inside.
"I know what we could do now," Little Bear said. "Visit Mr Beaver
and give him a big hug!"

"A brilliant idea, son!" said Daddy Bear. "It's sure to
brighten up his day."
And off they went. Along the way, they chatted
about how lucky they were to have one another. And
before they knew it, they had reached Mr Beaver's.

Mr Beaver was working so hard that Little Bear
and Daddy Bear danced to get his attention.
"Hello! We have come to hug you!" said Daddy Bear.
Mr Beaver was frightened. "Why?" he asked.
"To brighten up your day," said Little Bear.
So Mr Beaver agreed to a little hug. It felt
strange but nice.

"Dad, do you think Mr Beaver liked his hug?"
Little Bear asked.

"I think so," Daddy Bear replied. "Hugging always makes you feel good."

They were heading home when Little Bear pulled his dad's fur. "Can we hug someone else now?" he asked.

"Of course! Hugging is a fine way to spend your day!"
Daddy Bear smiled.

Miss Weasel was reading when she heard Little Bear.
"Excuse me, can we have a hug, please?"
Miss Weasel jumped. "You almost scared me to death!"
Little Bear apologised, then hugged Miss Weasel in
the most calming way he knew.

Next they met two hares eating fresh carrots.
"Ahem," Daddy Bear said. "May we try some of those?"
The hares froze. Not their precious carrots!
Daddy Bear nibbled one carrot. Little Bear nibbled another.

"I don't like these carrots much," said Daddy Bear.
"I don't either," said Little Bear. "I prefer hugs."
The hares were relieved. "If you'd prefer a hug
instead of a carrot, we'd be happy to help."

The Big Bad Wolf was
sharpening his claws.

"Have you seen a girl in a red hood?" he asked.

Daddy Bear shook his head.

Little Bear smiled. "We would like to give you a hug," he said.

The wolf looked at them suspiciously. "All right. But not too hard!"

The wolf enjoyed the hug so much, that he didn't notice
a little girl in a red hood skipping past.

By the stream, Old Mr Elk was having a drink.

"Would you mind if we gave you a hug?" Little Bear asked.

"But why hug an old beast like me?" Old Mr Elk said.

"Because it will make you feel good."

Old Mr Elk had to admit, Little Bear's hug *was* perfect.

In a clearing, a stranger was basking in the Sun.
"I didn't know that anacondas lived in our forest,"
said Daddy Bear.
Ms Anaconda hissed gently. "I'm visiting Grass Snake.
What are you doing?"
"We're hugging everyone we meet," Little Bear piped
up. "Would you like us to hug you?"
Ms Anaconda smiled. "It would be my pleasure."

Next they passed through a
meadow of sweet-smelling flowers,
and Little Bear shouted, "Look at that
colourful caterpillar! It's like a rainbow!"
Mrs Caterpillar sat up. "Out of my way!
I want to snuggle up in my cocoon."
"Could I give you one little hug
before you go to sleep?"
"Be quick!" said
Mrs Caterpillar.
So Little Bear hugged her
as quickly, and as delicately,
as he could.

Behind a bush, the bears spied a hunter.

Little Bear whispered: "Do you think we can hug him?"

"It would be rude not to," Daddy Bear replied.

So they picked up the hunter and hugged him hard.

"I will look after his net," said Daddy Bear.

On their way home, they hugged more animals.

"Hello, Mr Badger."

"This is cosy!"

"Ooh la la! What big muscles!"

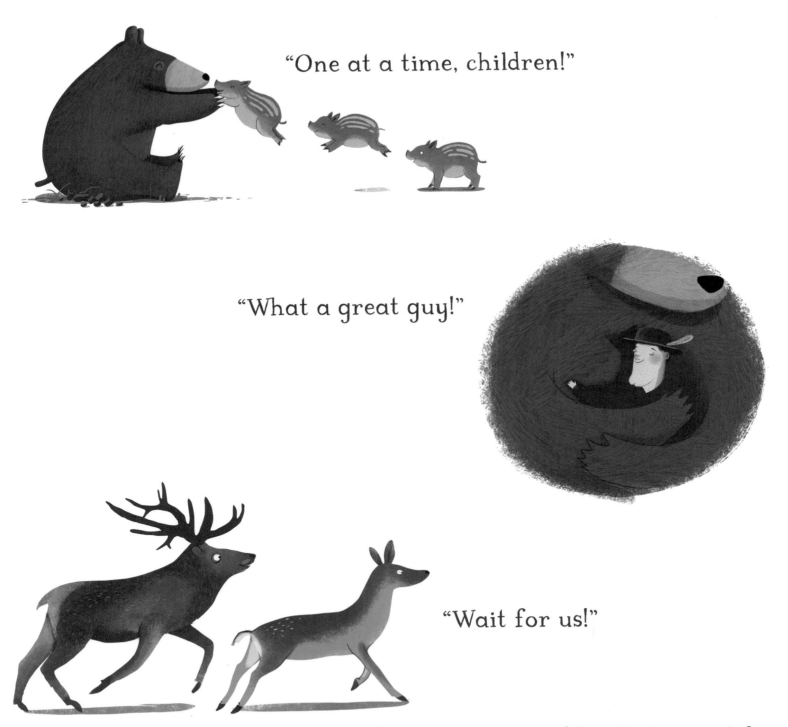

"One at a time, children!"

"What a great guy!"

"Wait for us!"

It was turning out to be one of the best days of Little Bear's life.

They were almost home when suddenly Little Bear sat down.

"Dad, haven't we forgotten someone?"

Daddy Bear stopped. He counted everyone who lived in the forest.

"I'm pretty sure we've hugged everyone."

"But Dad – think!"

Daddy Bear counted again. "I give up, son. Who have we missed?"

"Each other, Daddy!"

And they gave each other the strongest, hardest, longest, largest and most loving hug of all.

The End